Meet the Friends

Illustrated by Ameet Studio

SCHOLASTIC INC.

ISBN 978-0-545-59943-6

12 11 10 9 8 7 6 5 4 3 2 1   13 14 15 16 17 18/0

Printed in the U.S.A.   40
First printing, May 2013

Table of Contents

Welcome to Heartlake City

Meet Andrea, Mia, Emma, Olivia, and Stephanie. They're five best friends with unique personalities, and when they come together, they make the perfect team! Turn the page to learn fun facts about each girl, and then take the different quizzes to find out what makes your group of friends special.

Meet the Friends

Mia

Whether she's putting on a magic show or running in the school track meet, Mia loves being active. She enjoys playing all kinds of sports and practicing magic tricks to impress her friends. But if there's one thing Mia adores more than anything, it's animals. She's terrific with pets and even has her own horse, Bella.

While everyone has just five senses, Emma's friends swear that she has a sixth: fashion sense. With just a glance, Emma knows exactly how to make an outfit more glamorous, a room more colorful, or a painting more beautiful! She keeps her friends looking stylish, even when they're just hanging out in Olivia's tree house.

Emma

Andrea is a very talented singer, and she dreams of being a star someday! Whether she's rehearsing a new song or serving muffins at the café, she is always full of energy. Her friends say that she can be a bit dramatic sometimes, but what's life without a little excitement?

Andrea

Olivia

If there's a computer that needs fixing or an invention to be tinkered with, Olivia is the girl for the job. She can design and build almost anything—even a mini robot! She's also one of the funniest girls in Heartlake City. Her jokes always have the friends rolling with laughter.

Stephanie is outgoing and friendly, and loves working on group projects. When she's not hanging out, she's sure to be organizing something. Stephanie always has her notebook nearby to write down the week's schedule and make sure everything runs according to plan.

Stephanie

Heartlake City

One summer day, Heartlake City was hosting a World Petacular celebration. Mia, Andrea, Stephanie, Emma, and Olivia met there by accident, and they've been inseparable ever since! The five girls are all in the same grade at Heartlake High, so they're always working together on homework, planning school events, or heading to sports games. Most weekends they hang out at the City Park Café. But if they're not there, you'll be sure to find them up in Olivia's tree house, sharing stories and secrets.

Perfect Pets

Each of the friends has her very own pet that matches her personality purr-fectly! Read about their cute animals, and then decide which pet would be your perfect companion.

❧ Charlie

Charlie is Mia's very curious—and very hungry—puppy. Mia spends hours playing fetch with him in the park. When she doesn't have her eye on him, he often gets into mischief by chasing butterflies or sneaking treats from picnic baskets.

❧ Kitty

Stephanie's white cat, Kitty, adores naps in the sunshine or chasing balls of yarn. Whenever Stephanie feels stressed about event planning, Kitty is there with an extra nuzzle. It doesn't hurt that Stephanie usually has a treat or two on hand as well!

❖ Sunshine

Emma was nervous about learning to ride horses at the Heartlake Stables. But all that changed when she met Sunshine. Gentle and patient, Sunshine was cantering with Emma in no time. And Emma enjoys brushing Sunshine's silky mane.

❖ Oscar

Oscar the hedgehog's prickly nature is the perfect match for Andrea's spunky personality. He's not the cuddliest pet in the world, but he likes listening to Andrea's new song lyrics. And Andrea makes sure to give him lots of attention, too.

❖ Maxie

When Olivia first moved to Heartlake City, it took her a little while to make friends. Until she did, Maxie helped her feel right at home. This sweet kitten loves to explore and climb on new things. Olivia quickly created plenty of inventive cat toys to keep Maxie busy!

Which pet would match your personality best?

Stephanie

About Me

Quote: "Everything's under control . . . almost!"

Favorite activities: Party planning and writing

Favorite books: Fantasy novels

Someday I want to be: An author

What my friends say about me: "We trust Stephanie to keep us on time . . . and keep a secret!"

Best Memory

One time, a new book from my favorite author was about to go on sale. I'd been looking forward to buying it for weeks! I even helped the store plan a book party to celebrate. Little did I know, my friends planned a surprise, too. They invited the author to my party, and she signed my copy! It was the best night ever.

Secret Tricks

When Mia performed a magic show in the school talent festival, I was her assistant. She swore me to secrecy about her card tricks. To this day, I haven't told anyone how she did them. I wanted her to know she could trust me. When someone asks me about them, I just say, "It was magic!"

Can You Be Trusted?

Take this quiz to find out if you're a trustworthy friend like Stephanie!

Your friend tells you a secret. What do you do?

A I'd only tell my close friends. But I'd swear them to secrecy, too.

B I would never tell anyone. My friend can trust me.

C If it was really a secret, then my friend would never have shared it. So it's okay to spill.

My friends:

A tell me simply everything about themselves!

B ask me for advice with tough problems.

C know it's sometimes difficult for me to hold my tongue.

If I make a promise to a friend:

A I try to stick to it. But I make so many promises, it's hard to keep track!

B I always come through, even if I have to cancel other plans.

C I intend to keep it, but sometimes forget.

I have:

A loads of friends, and we talk about everything. And everyone.

B a small group of close friends.

C many people I hang out with but don't consider "true" friends.

Now count which answer you have chosen the most and see if people can trust you.

Mostly As: You're very outgoing and friendly, and a bit of a social butterfly. However, you sometimes reveal too much or make promises you can't keep.

> **GOOD ADVICE:** If your friend tells you a secret, remember that she trusts you to keep it. And maybe only make a few promises, rather than a lot. That way, you can follow through on the ones that count.

Mostly Bs: You are the queen of keeping quiet. When somebody tells you a secret, your lips are zipped. You always keep your promises, and you expect others to do the same.

> **GOOD ADVICE:** Don't stress too much about being the keeper of everyone's secrets. Sometimes, you have to give yourself a break, too!

Mostly Cs: Many people are always around because you have juicy gossip to share. But spilling secrets makes it hard for others to trust you.

> **GOOD ADVICE:** Being popular by spreading interesting news isn't the same as having close friends. Try sticking with a small group of friends and sharing fewer secrets. Your friendships will be much stronger!

Mia

About Me

Quote: "Let's get to work!"

Favorite activities: Horseback riding, magic tricks

Favorite books: Stories about animals

Someday I want to be: A veterinarian

What my friends say about me: "Sometimes we think Mia might like animals more than people." 😊

Going for Gold

This is my horse, Bella. We enter lots of riding competitions together. Another rider named Lacy and her horse, Gingersnap, are our main competitors. We don't always win, but I know I can count on Bella to do her best!

If I Were Writing a Story . . .

I'd probably write an adventure about animals living in a magical world . . . where they could talk! My dog, Charlie, barks when he's hungry, and Bella nuzzles me when she wants attention. But I'd love to really be able to talk to animals. Imagine all the cool things they'd have to say!

What's Your Perfect Pet?

If you could have any pet, what would it be? Take this quiz to find out which animal resembles you the most!

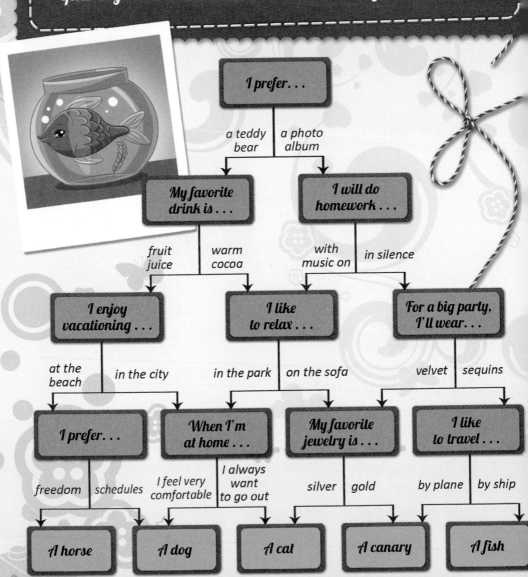

I prefer...

a teddy bear — a photo album

My favorite drink is... / **I will do homework...**

fruit juice — warm cocoa — with music on — in silence

I enjoy vacationing... / **I like to relax...** / **For a big party, I'll wear...**

at the beach — in the city — in the park — on the sofa — velvet — sequins

I prefer... / **When I'm at home...** / **My favorite jewelry is...** / **I like to travel...**

freedom — schedules — I feel very comfortable — I always want to go out — silver — gold — by plane — by ship

A horse / **A dog** / **A cat** / **A canary** / **A fish**

A Horse

You're fond of nature, just like Mia. You dislike too many rules and can sometimes be a bit bossy. So your ideal animal is a horse. Together you would gallop off into the sunset. Maybe it's time for you to visit the nearest stable?

A Dog

You are hardworking and loyal, just like Stephanie. You spend your free time doing outdoor activities, but you also like for things to be on schedule. The perfect pet for you is a dog! Together you can spend hours playing outside and taking walks.

A Cat

You enjoy freedom and doing things on your own, but you also like knowing you can count on close friends for support. Just like Olivia, the perfect pet for you is a cat—this animal may seem to be a loner, but it also likes to be cuddled and stroked.

A Bird

Music fills almost every part of your life. This makes you very similar to Andrea, and your perfect pet should love music as much as you! Your best choice would be a bird who will sing sweet tunes. Who knows? Maybe one day you will perform a duet.

A Fish

Though you like animals, you're not exactly a "pet person." You enjoy designing cute pet outfits more than actually playing a game of fetch. The perfect choice for you would be a fish. You could admire its colors and decorate its tank with accessories!

Olivia

About Me

Quote: "It's easy! Or at least, we can figure it out."

Favorite activities: Inventions, photography

Favorite books: Textbooks

Someday I want to be: A scientist

What my friends say about me: "We count on Olivia for awesome inventions . . . and help with our homework."

My Tree House

One of my favorite spots is the tree house in my backyard. My friends come over to hang out here, eat snacks, and share stories. One time, we had a sleepover all weekend. My parents brought us up food and blankets so we could stay in the tree house all night.

Funniest Story

Last year, we were assigned a school science project to come up with a new invention. My friends couldn't believe it when I designed a vacuum cleaner that played music! But when the vacuum was on, you couldn't hear the song. So it was back to the drawing board.

Friendship Test

The five friends know they can have fun together and rely on one another whenever they need a helping hand. Are you a reliable friend? Take this quiz to find out!

What do you do when:

Your friend is sick. Do you:
- Visit her and cheer her up. ✳✳✳
- Tell her about the good times you're having with your other friends. ✳
- Take notes in class for her so she doesn't fall behind. ✳✳

You only have one chocolate bar, and your friend sits down next to you. Do you:
- Give it to your friend. You don't really like chocolate, anyway. ✳✳
- Quickly eat it! ✳
- Divide it in half and share it with your friend. ✳✳✳

Your friend wants to perform in the school karaoke contest, but she's not a great singer. Do you:
- Give her some pointers. ✳✳
- Sing with her. It'll be fun if you're together! ✳✳✳
- Laugh when she can't hit all the notes. ✳

Your friend is taking part in the same race as you. Do you:

- Let her think she's winning. Then cut in front of her right at the finish line. ✶
- Let her win. ✶✶
- Enjoy the race and cheer her on no matter which one of you wins. ✶✶✶

When your friend tells you her biggest secret, do you:

- Tell her a secret in return. ✶✶
- Let her know her secret is safe with you. ✶✶✶
- Tell your other friends the moment she's gone! ✶

From 5 to 7 ✶

Hmm . . . friendship is not your strongest point. But it's something you can work on! They next time you're with your friend, try to put her needs ahead of your own. And pay a bit more attention to her feelings. You'll be a great friend in no time!

From 8 to 11 ✶

You are very helpful, and everyone likes being around you. You take care of your friend and do everyting for her. However, don't forget to think about yourself sometimes, too. Friendship is about being happy together!

From 12 to 15 ✶

Having you as a friend is like winning the jackpot. You are a very reliable person, and you are always there for your friend—no matter what. You share everything together, and your friendship makes you both stronger.

Emma

About Me

Quote: "That is so you!"

Favorite activities: Drawing, sewing

Favorite books: Fashion magazines

Someday I want to be: A costume designer

What my friends say about me: "Emma, come quick. We need a makeover!"

Picture-Perfect

My friends and I were helping out at a kindergarten art camp one summer. The campers wanted to draw our pictures, so we fixed our hair and posed while they colored. We thought we looked pretty cool, but the drawings turned out different than we expected! My friends and I still laugh every time we look at them.

Emma's Fashion Tips

It's fun showcasing your personality with fashion. I always tell my friends, just take a little extra time in the morning to do something special. Try a new hairstyle. Wear a colorful belt or bracelet. Even paint your fingernails. Fashion is about expressing yourself.

What's Your Personality?

Take this quiz with your friends to find out what roles you play in your group.

In the shopping mall:

A I always have a shopping list.
B I can't wait to leave.
C I rush to the bookstore.
D I hang out at the coffee shop.
E I help my friends carry their bags.

The accessory that suits me best is:

A A digital watch
B A tool kit
C A camera
D A colorful MP3 player
E A glittery lip balm

In a school performance:

A I'm the director.
B I design the set.
C I run the sound board.
D I play the leading role.
E I make the costumes.

The perfect symbol to describe me would be:

 A B C D E

Now count which answer you have chosen most often and see which role you play in your group of friends!

 Mostly As:

A Master of Organization:

If there's a party to be planned or a meeting to be held, you're there one minute early with a list of things to do. Just remember to have fun while you're doing all that scheduling.

Mostly Bs:

A Handy Girl: You are the go-to girl everyone relies on when something needs to be moved, built, or repaired. Your friends appreciate your help—and admire how handy you are.

Mostly Cs:

A Thinker: Complicated calculations? A new invention? You can't wait to get started! You are very smart and are always thinking of ways to improve things—or reinvent them!

Mostly Ds:

A Star: Do you sing along with every song on the radio? Are you the first in line for musical tryouts? You were born to perform! Thanks to your outgoing personality, you make friends easily and make their lives more colorful.

Mostly Es:

A Fashionista: You enjoy tasks the most when they require artistic expertise. Your outfits look perfect each day, you always know which colors go best together, and your friends come to you for makeovers.

Andrea

About Me

Quote: "Music puts life in full color!"

Favorite activities: Singing, acting

Favorite books: Movie scripts

Someday I want to be: An actress or musician

What my friends say about me: "We've already asked Andrea for her autograph because we know she'll be a star someday!"

Most Embarrassing Moment

Our school was holding auditions for a new musical. I couldn't wait to try out! I practiced my audition for weeks. But on the big night, I accidently went to the wrong classroom. A debate tournament was going on, and I didn't realize it. When I sang to the audience, they were completely confused!

Rock Star

Do you want to write a song with me? It will be fun! Just fill in the blanks.

No matter where I am, on sea or _____,

My friends are there to lend a _____.

Together, we can do _____,

as long as there are songs to _____!

Answers: land, hand, anything, sing

Quiz:

It's Showtime!

Take this quiz with your friends to see what type of movie you should each star in.

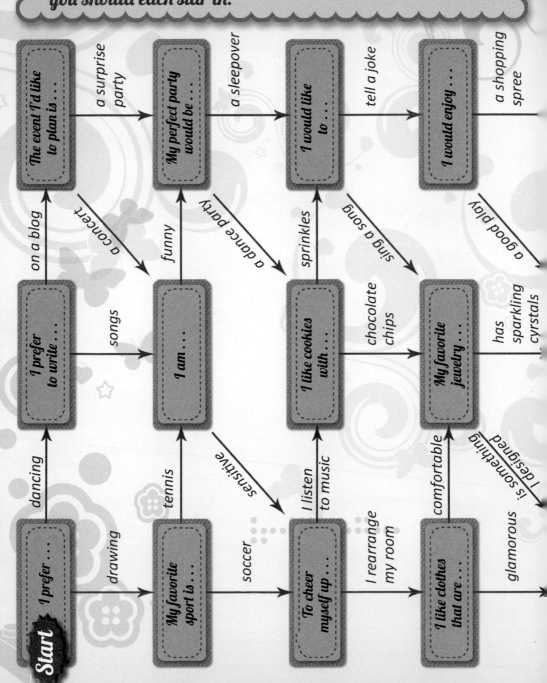

Start

I prefer . . .

The event I'd like to plan is . . . — a surprise party

My perfect party would be . . . — a sleepover

I would like to . . . — tell a joke

I would enjoy . . . — a shopping spree

on a blog

a concert

I prefer to write . . . — songs

I am . . . — funny

a dance party

sprinkles

I like cookies with . . . — chocolate chips

sing a song

My favorite jewelry . . . — has sparkling cyrstals

a good play

dancing

drawing

tennis

sensitive

My favorite sport is . . . — soccer

I listen to music

To cheer myself up . . . — I rearrange my room

comfortable

I like clothes that are . . . — glamorous

is something I designed

has sparkling cyrstals

Comedy

You are extremely open and sociable. Your friends think you are the life and soul of every party. The best film role for you would be a comedy. Your great sense of humor would have everyone laughing at every scene!

Musical

Does your heart beat faster at the very thought of singing, dancing, or acting? Then why not connect all three? Your ideal movie role would be the leading lady in a musical. Everyone admires your talent, and you're sure to steal the spotlight.

Drama

You like to stand out from the crowd and create different styles for every occasion. In a drama, you'd have the chance to play multiple roles . . . and wear many gorgeous costumes! The only thing you might like better would be designing the costumes instead.

Thanks for hanging out with us!

We hope you've enjoyed getting to know each of us better. Now it's time to create new adventures with your own group of friends. We can't wait to hear about them the next time you stop by!